The Bumper Christmas Book of Fascinating Facts about Brussel Sprouts

BY James Stevens

Gemmi Fera

Bookaful Press

1. They are fart bombs
2. They are green and round
3. It is a great ketchup
4. They are delicious a traditional
5. They are bubble and squeak
   food like